Copyright © 1988 David P. Makhanlall
Illustrations © 1988 Amelia Rosato
First published 1988 by Blackie and Son Ltd

British Library Cataloguing in Publication Data
Makhanlall, David
Brer Anansi and the boat race, —
(Folk-tales of the world).
I. Title   II. Rosato, Amelia   III. Series
813 [J]   PZ7
ISBN 0-216-92355-7

Blackie and Son Ltd
7 Leicester Place
London WC2H 7BP

First American edition published in 1988 by
Peter Bedrick Books
125 East 23rd Street
New York NY 10010

Library of Congress Cataloging-in-Publication Data

Makhanlall, David P.
Brer Anansi and the boat race/David P. Makhanlall; pictures by
Amelia Rosato. — 1st American ed.
p. cm. — (Folk tales of the world)
"A Caribbean folk tale."
Summary: Brer Anansi uses a boat race with Brer Rabbit and Brer
Bear as an opportunity to perform his usual mischief.
ISBN 0-87226-184-0
1. Anansi (Legendary character) [1. Anansi (Legendary character)
2. Folklore — West Indies.] I. Rosato, Amelia, ill. II. Title.
III. Series: Folk tales of the world (New York. N.Y.)
PZ8. 1.M292Bo 1988
398.2′452544—dc19
[E]

Printed in Italy

Brer Anansi and The Boat Race

David P. Makhanlall

Pictures by Amelia Rosato

A Caribbean Folk Tale
Blackie

It had been raining non-stop for three days. There was water everywhere. Mr Thunder was in one of his moods. He seemed determined to flood Animal Land in his anger.

'I don't know what Mr Thunder is up to,' remarked Brer Weasel as he stood looking out of his window, 'but if the rains continue for another two or three days, we will all be swimming for our lives.'

Although Brer Rabbit's burrow was flooded and Brer Bear's house had three inches of water, the two friends were not finding it too difficult. They were both now living in Brer Rabbit's boat. It had a sort of tent over it. They ate, slept, cooked and washed in the boat.

Brer Anansi, meanwhile, sat next to his fire. He was wrapped in three blankets and sat drinking hot tea.

'My house is up a tree,' said Anansi to himself. 'It can rain non-stop for a month and I will still be safe.'

'Ho there, Anansi!'

Brer Anansi went to his window and opened it a little. He looked down below at the boat.

'Ah, so you are all warm wrapped up in your blanket,' said Brer Rabbit.

'While we are having a wonderful time in our boat!' boasted Brer Bear.

Brer Anansi said nothing. He looked at his enemies' boat. Indeed, they were having a grand time. Where was his boat?

'Your boat floated away an hour ago,' said Brer Rabbit. 'We saw it go by as we were doing our washing. Too bad. You'll have to stay at home while me and Brer Bear go see the world.'

'See you around, pal!' shouted Brer Rabbit, and he and Brer
Bear sailed off in the rain.

'I'll teach them! Show-offs!' muttered Brer Anansi. 'I too have
a boat!'

Brer Anansi got his bath-tub out. It was shaped like an egg but
had a flat bottom. It would float quite nicely. He had to get a top
for it or the rain would come in.

Anansi took one of his potted plants and set it up in the middle
of the tub. Then he tied his umbrella to the plant. The umbrella
was quite large and would cover the whole tub.

Brer Anansi climbed in and sailed out into the rain after his two enemies.

Brer Bear was the first to spot him. 'There! Brer Anansi is after us!'

'After us?' asked Brer Rabbit. 'That's a lie! He is at home sleeping!'

Brer Rabbit looked up from under the tent. His eyes nearly popped out of his head when he saw Brer Anansi in his 'boat'.

'How about a race?' asked Brer Bear.

'Okay!' Brer Anansi steadied himself. The boats were now level.

'Go!' cried Brer Rabbit.

The race was on!

But after ten minutes, they decided to stop. They were all tired.

'We can't go fast enough because of our supplies and things,' said Brer Rabbit. 'Or else we would have won quite easily.'

'Why don't you unload your boat?' said Brer Anansi.

'That's an idea,' said Brer Rabbit. 'But our supplies would be ruined.'

'Not necessarily so,' said Brer Anansi. 'You may use your table. You can set it up in the water. Then you can pile your supplies onto it.'

'Say,' said Brer Rabbit, 'that's grand. A sort of island!'

So Brer Bear and Brer Rabbit set their table up in the water and piled everything onto it.

Then they took their small tub and filled it with their supplies. This they tied to one of the legs of the table with strong cord. The tub lay floating next to the table.

They were now all set to race with Brer Anansi!

The race was on! Both boats were going quite fast. However, Brer Rabbit's boat was getting slowly ahead. First, it was one inch, then two inches, then three inches and then four inches .

'Yahoo!' screamed Brer Bear. 'We're winning!'

Indeed, they were winning. Brer Anansi and his bath-tub appeared to have vanished.

Then it stopped raining quite suddenly.

Brer Rabbit and Brer Bear stopped paddling and their boat came to a stop. They looked at each other in silence. What had happened to Brer Anansi?

'Let's go back and see. Perhaps he sank!'

'Ho-ho!' cried Brer Bear. 'He must have pulled the plug of the tub out! Ho-ho!'

They searched among all the 'island-bushes' but they could not find Brer Anansi. Then they got tired and decided to go for their supplies.

But they could only find their table!

The tub of supplies was not there.

'I know what,' said Brer Rabbit. 'Brer Anansi has run off with our supplies!'

'Let's go to his house!' said Brer Rabbit. 'We shall teach him a lesson or two!'

They came to Brer Anansi's house and started to shout all sorts of things about him.

But there was no answer from the silent, closed house.

Where was Brer Anansi? Did his bath-tub sink? Did he drown?

'We will miss Anansi,' said Brer Rabbit.

'Will you?'

They turned around. There was Anansi sailing peacefully about in his bath-tub.

'Ah, there you are!' screamed Brer Bear. 'Why did you run off with our supplies?'

'Run off with your supplies?' asked Brer Anansi, quite innocently. 'I do not know what you are talking about.'

'Did you look where you had left them?' said Brer Anansi.

'We did,' answered Brer Bear. 'They are not there!'

'Then someone must have taken them!'

'A likely story,' said Brer Rabbit. 'If it did happen then that person must be you!'

'I'll tell you the truth,' said Brer Anansi. 'When I started racing with you, I realized that you would win. I went towards my house. I arrived home, and *there*! as I looked out my window I saw your tub of supplies floating by. The string must have broken free!'

'One of Brer Alligator's laws says that any belongings floating in the sea without the owner around are free property. Anyone finding any floating object can claim it. Under that law I claim your tub of supplies.'

Brer Rabbit looked at Brer Bear and Brer Bear looked at Brer Rabbit.

'Anansi!' shouted Brer Rabbit. 'I know that you cut the cord!'

Brer Anansi did not answer. He turned his tub around and headed for home. Both Brer Rabbit and Brer Bear looked at their tub of supplies tied to the end of Anansi's boat.

'After him!'

They started to paddle but they soon got stuck in the mud.

And Brer Anansi went home and drank his tea by the fire.